THIS IS THE FIRST BOOK I WILL READ TO YOU

BY Francesco Sedita

ILLUSTRATED BY Magenta Fox

VIKING

This is the first book I will read to you,
my sweet child.

After we take our bath,

I'll put you in your softest pajamas.

And wrap you in your blanket.

You'll wiggle your feet and squirm
as I hold you.

And I'll be nervous—
to share this moment that only you and I will be a part of.

You might not want to listen at first.

Maybe you'll want to be doing something else.

But then we'll find our way together.

You'll rest comfortably in my arms
as my voice becomes gentler, quieter.

In our hearts we'll know that
this is the first book I will read to you.

This is our book.

I'll hold you close and
turn each page gently,
reading to you in a voice
as soft as the blanket
you're wrapped in.

We have stories to discover and magical places to visit, you and I.

But tonight, this is the first book I'll read to you.

You'll rest in the crook of my arm and the moon will shine on us.

And the world will stop.

The winds won't howl, the trees won't rustle, the air will sit still.

All for now, for this precious moment . . .

It's only us.

Me and you.

Just these words.

Just this book.

No worries from this difficult but beautiful world.

No doubts, no sadness.
This time is our time.

And no matter how big you are,
I will always be here to hold you.

Only the click of this lamp,
the sounds of our house,
the touch of our hands.

The blue moonlight.

And then, when you fall asleep,
I'll turn the last page.

And tuck you in,
and kiss your face.

And before I leave you,
I'll lose my breath as I look into your crib
and remember this moment always.

This book is for my mother, Rochelle, who once told me that peeking into my room and seeing
me in the crib was like seeing me for the first time, every time. She instilled a love of reading and
writing in me. And read *Charlotte's Web* to me time and again. "It is not often that someone
comes along who is a true friend and a good writer. Charlotte was both." —E. B. White
—F. S.

For Nanette, Ephram, Amelia, and Georgiana
—M. F.

VIKING
An imprint of Penguin Random House LLC, New York

First published in the United States of America by Viking, an imprint of Penguin Random House LLC, 2023

Visit us online at penguinrandomhouse.com.

Library of Congress Cataloging-in-Publication Data is available.

Manufactured in China

ISBN 9780593405055

TOPL

Design by Opal Roengchai
Text set in Recoleta Medium
The illustrations were created digitally.